About the Author

I was intrigued by Japanese culture and mythology from a young age. Growing up watching anime series and reading many books about Japan sparked a huge interest and curiosity especially for Japanese mythology. I am very passionate about art in general and everything that brings inner joy and self-awareness, but at the same time I always look for things that help me to know myself better.

The Magpie and the Tree of Life

Nicolae Raluca-Georgiana

The Magpie and the Tree of Life

Olympia Publishers
London

www.olympiapublishers.com
OLYMPIA PAPERBACK EDITION

Copyright © Nicolae Raluca-Georgiana 2022

The right of Nicolae Raluca-Georgiana to be identified as author of this work has been asserted in accordance with sections 77 and 78 of the Copyright, Designs and Patents Act 1988.

All Rights Reserved

No reproduction, copy or transmission of this publication may be made without written permission.
No paragraph of this publication may be reproduced, copied or transmitted save with the written permission of the publisher, or in accordance with the provisions of the Copyright Act 1956 (as amended).

Any person who commits any unauthorised act in relation to this publication may be liable to criminal prosecution and civil claims for damage.

A CIP catalogue record for this title is available from the British Library.

ISBN: 978-1-80074-811-8

This is a work of fiction.
Names, characters, places and incidents originate from the writer's imagination. Any resemblance to actual persons, living or dead, is purely coincidental.

First Published in 2022

Olympia Publishers
Tallis House
2 Tallis Street
London
EC4Y 0AB

Printed in Great Britain

Chapter 1

Shinsei village and its heritage

It was late autumn in Japan.
    The rain had stopped.
    All of the leaves from the tree crowns were shining in the light of the sun that emerged from the clouds, ruby red, peach orange and citrine yellow were just a few of the nuances nature had to offer. It was a treat for both mind and soul.
    You could hear from far away the sound of the river and see birds flying from tree to tree, foxes chasing their next meal, and humans going about their day-to-day lives.
    The village of Shinsei was located in the mountainous area of Japan, a place that holds many legends of beings from supernatural realms, both good and bad.
    It was a not a place for weak souls.
    Many people who had the gift of craftmanship, or that wanted to learn the art of healing the human body, were inspired to become artisans, bladesmiths and shamans.
    The mélange of both rough tasks and delicate ones was in perfect balance thanks to the practical mindset of the villagers; for them it came naturally to offer and receive help when needed.
    They had only each other in one of the hardest places to live on Earth.
    To be able to survive and thrive in Shinsei village took a lot of hard work, but also a good amount of wisdom.

The people that lived here respected nature and knew that she came first, so they took with caution every task that could affect it.

Shinsei village had one of the best gifts from the Universe — a gingko biloba tree in its full splendor.

Many people still wonder to this day how could this tree evolve in such rough conditions; they knew that its presence could not be taken for granted, as all good things in life for that matter...

Even though the village was blessed with magnific surroundings, a part of its history was very dark.

A horrible disease came upon their village, many people had gone mad and after that they disappeared from the face of the earth.

The people from the surrounding villages thought the hunger caused by the lack of harvest or the floods that took their homes made them lose their mind, but not all things are as they seem to be...

The souls of Shinsei prayed that their beloved realm would remain protected from all fear and events that could cause harm to it.

Chapter 2

Maru and Sakura

The day started as usual for Sakura.

She washed herself, put her kimono on, and ate some noodles that her grandmother made for her.

Her little friend, Maru (a fluffy chinchilla) was waiting patiently for her to finish.

He was a naughty little bastard.

Whenever she would leave the table, he would steal some food and hide it for later.

Even though Maru had bad habits, Sakura knew that whenever things got serious, she could rely on the little creature, so his occasional cheekiness was forgotten.

After she finished eating, Sakura placed Maru on her shoulder, took her bag and went for a walk.

She loved to walk barefoot, especially in autumn when the soil was wet from the rain.

She was at peace when she felt the earth under her feet.

Sakura would go often to "the tree of life", as the villagers called it, to pick up leaves and fruit from it to make natural medicine for the villagers; she was the youngest healer, but a very determined one.

Her relationship with the tree was a special one.

She sometimes felt as if the tree could sense her fears and worries and it would respond by calming her down with its energy.

After she prepared the medicine, Sakura went to each house to treat the souls that needed help.

For the villagers, she truly was like a freshly-blossomed cherry flower. They enjoyed her calm energy and charismatic nature.

She knew she had a great responsibility; many people relied on her.

She was born in a family with a long line of healers.

Her ancestors vowed to protect nature and to help humans in need.

This inspired her to become a healer.

Although it was not an easy task, by all means, it was vital for the fate of her birthplace.

After treating all of the villagers who needed her help, Sakura went home and rested.

Of course, her naughty little friend had to do something cheeky and started chewing the papers she used for her journal.

She pretended she was sleeping so she could observe him.

Her guilty pleasure was to look at this perfectly round ball of fur and laugh at his shenanigans.

She thought often about how her little friend taught her something that would remain with her forever — how to see the light in people even when they are filled with darkness...

She missed her parents every day and wondered what really happened to them.

Sakura never asked for anything until now. She wanted to find them and recover the years spent without their presence.

Chapter 3

Matsuko's wisdom

Matsuko was standing in front of the house drinking tea.

She was waiting for her granddaughter to arrive.

She reminisced that when she was sixteen, her mother told her, unfortunate events happen in order for people to learn to appreciate the good in their lives.

When she was older, she understood, blessings cannot exist without unfortunate events; there cannot be good without evil.

The key is learning how to tame the chaos; how to use it to your advantage in order to conquer evil.

This was passed on to Sakura when she was old enough to understand matters of existence.

Matsuko knew that the peace the villagers felt wouldn't last for long…

Dark clouds were appearing in the sky, but they weren't from natural causes.

She sensed that something from the underworld was lingering in the air.

Soon everything was about to change.

It was a matter of time.

Her granddaughter arrived to give her the treatment she needed.

Matsuko was looking at Sakura when a disturbing thought appeared in her mind, innocence could be a huge disadvantage for Sakura if this part of her was not dealt with.

The world is full of humans or creatures that prey on the innocent.

Little did she know that soon enough the fate of the entire region would depend on Sakura.

The hardest question Matsuko had to ask herself was, "Will she remain the same after seeing the real face of humanity?"

Sakura's innocence and stubborn nature made her who she was.

Her grandmother knew this very well…

Chapter 4

Takumi's courage

In the past, Sakura's grandfather, Takumi, was a respectable blacksmith.

Samurai from all over Japan came to him.

His level of craftmanship in the art of sword-making was almost from another world.

He learned this art form at a very young age.

He had no choice.

His family was very poor.

When he was a child, his father died from tuberculosis.

Although Takumi was devastated, as one would expect, he did not let this tragic event end his life.

He started spending time at the sword-maker's shop.

The blacksmith grew fond of the little boy and allowed him to observe the process of making a sword.

The first years as a blacksmith were very difficult for Takumi.

The inner pressure he felt was huge.

He knew that if he were to fail, his whole family would have been in a very difficult situation.

They could not afford food or clothes for the cold season.

What would happen to his family was a terrifying thought to Takumi.

He felt compelled to save them.

The death of his father had awoken something inside of him that was beyond anything he could ever imagine, a power in which he never had the "audacity" to believe.

He had no other choice, he had to fight for his mother.

He was the only one that had the endurance needed to help his mother survive this period that felt almost like a curse for her.

She was not ready to leave yet...

Years passed and Takumi's knowledge expanded.

He felt blessed for the opportunity he was given.

Takumi knew that it had to be a greater power involved in this drastic life change that he fully embraced not only for the sake of his family, but for his future also.

When his mother became old, she told him that he would become an important element in the puzzle of life; Takumi became very curious, but the riddle was yet to be solved.

After three months his mother died of old age, soon after he met Matsuko.

Takumi was twenty-eight years old when he met her.

Matsuko was a gorgeous young woman with long black hair, her skin was smooth like ivory and her eyes were hazel brown.

The moment they met would become crucial for Takumi's future; he had lost his sense of purpose after his parents died.

Matsuko would become his crescent star from the night sky.

She shined in everything she did.

Matsuko helped him in all aspects of life.

Takumi felt as if the Universe blessed him one more time.

Although Matsuko felt a sense of inner peace and a small dose of pride that Takumi considered her an important aspect of his life, she never let this influence her judgement; she always remained modest and grateful for the blessing Takumi offered her, their lovely daughter.

Before giving birth, Matsuko told Takumi that she felt something interesting during her pregnancy, it was like the baby had some kind of a special aura, that protected him from evil; something that she also sensed in Takumi; Matsuko had the ability to sense when various entities were coming nearby their house, but when they came too close to Takumi, they suddenly disappeared…

Chapter 5

Yukimo

Takumi and Matsuko's daughter, Yukimo, was a very sensible child.

When she was a young lady, her parents noticed that every time she went in the village to go for her daily walks, she would always offer help to the villagers.

Matsuko sensed that someday she would become a healer.

When that day came, her parents were very happy that she had chosen a life path that involved helping people find peace in their mind and bodies.

Although sometimes Yukimo came home exhausted, she loved the path she had chosen and vowed to never let anything disturb her life journey.

She loved to learn new techniques and recipes that would help the people from her village.

In the same time, she was careful not to ignore the needs of her parents, who were getting older day by day.

Chapter 6

Yukimo and Kazuno meet

In order to help the villagers, Yukimo had to cross very steep areas.

Because Shinsei village was situated in the mountains, there were many dangerous areas where many people lost their lives.

Yukimo knew that humans were just a particle of dust in the Universe.

She never took for granted how precious life was and how easily one can lose it.

She had to cross a wooden bridge every day in order to reach the other side of the village.

Although she knew the danger involved, at the same time she always reminded herself that there were many old or sick people for whom the treatment she gave was vital.

When she almost reached the other end of the wooden bridge, she heard a disturbing noise, the timber started to rip apart.

Yukimo was horrified of what was about to happen in that second, the image of her parents appeared in her head and how they would react when hearing that she had died on that bridge that should have been replaced many years ago, but the villagers were too afraid to go there, because it was said that the bridge was filled with the spirits of the dead that lost their lives there.

Yukimo managed to grab a rope that was hanging from a

tree, but she knew that she could disappear in a second forever.

In the moment her hand lost the grip of the rope, she felt that something grabbed her and after, she was on the ground again.

Whoever or whatever saved her, had disappeared.

She could not believe that she was still alive after she came so close to her death.

She knew that this was a sign that her life purpose was not over yet; something was keeping her here.

After she calmed herself, she returned to the village and told her parents what had happened.

As expected, they were shocked, but at the same they were extremely grateful that Yukimo came out alive from this situation.

The villagers built a new bridge after this, a more solid one.

After twenty-three days, a new figure appeared in the village.

It was a tall man with long hair and a scar on his face, named Kazuno.

He was looking for a healer.

His wounds were still fresh from being attacked by something that he could not distinguish; it was nighttime.

He somehow managed to escape, but he was full of deep cuts.

When he met Yukimo, he was intrigued by her.

She was a fragile woman, but at the same time, her interior strength appealed to him.

He liked that she was a capable woman, but also an empathic one.

When Yukimo was cleaning Kazuno's wounds, she noticed that he had huge claw marks on his back and chest.

She wondered what animal was capable of doing such

damage to a human.

Yukimo thought it was probably a brown bear.

She asked the man if he saw what creature attacked him, but unfortunately everything happened too fast for him to realize what it was.

Yukimo became a bit worried because of the big possibility that whatever attacked Kazuno could have followed the path his blood left, was lurking somewhere in the surroundings, and could attack the villagers in any moment.

Months had passed and nothing significant happened, except the fact that Kazuno became very fond of Yukimo.

He asked her to teach him how to heal people.

Kazuno wanted to understand what it was about the art of healing people that Yukimo loved so much.

Soon after he understood.

Yukimo loved the fact that her actions had a significant effect on raising the quality of people's life and at the same time she could ease their mind and body; she made them feel less pain.

She wasn't doing this for the gratification.

Yukimo wanted to live in a world with less suffering.

Many people considered her an idealist for seeing the world like this, but she didn't give a damn.

She knew her purpose in life.

Chapter 7

Feelings emerge

Kazuno became more and more attracted to Yukimo.
    The feeling was mutual for her too.
    She sometimes observed Kazuno's figure and how calm he was in every situation.
    Yukimo was almost fascinated by him.
    You could have sensed immediately the attraction they had for each other.
    It was like a game of cat and mouse between them.
    Although Kazuno sometimes was feeling impatient, he remained respectful and allowed Yukimo to take her time, and most important, to feel safe around him.
    In the end, they allowed themselves to enjoy each other and something magic happened soon after…

Chapter 8

Sakura's birth

At the beginning of April, their child was born.

They named her Sakura.

Yukimo was very fond of this name.

She loved to see how magnificent the cherry trees were in spring.

It was Yukimo's favorite time of the year.

Sakura had the resilience of her father and the kindness of her mother.

She knew how to be strong, yet sensible at the same time.

But what was reserved for her would change her life forever…

Chapter 9

Shinsei's village dark period

Soon after Sakura came into the world, the village was attacked by beings from supernatural realms.

An army of yokai had disturbed the village's peace and terrorized the people.

A lot of them died after the attacks and the villagers who escaped ended up with serious wounds and had gone mad from what they had witnessed and disappeared; they could not bear everything that was happening.

Many people thought this was the doing of Hira, an evil woman with a single purpose on earth, to bring terror and suffering into the human world.

At first it was believed that Hira was a woman like many others that lived in Shinsei village.

At that time, she was a cook and worked very hard for her child.

Hira's only goal at that point was to offer her child everything she could not have.

The child grew, and became a responsible young man; he helped his mother with everything she needed and loved to study.

When he was sixteen, his mother sent him to get some supplies for her.

He never came back.

Hira was devastated.

She became full of hatred and grief and blamed the villagers for the disappearance of her son.

She could not accept the fact that nobody saw her son before his disappearance and in her eyes, nobody showed compassion for the unfortunate event.

Hira disappeared from Shinsei village in order to find her son.

She summoned the help of various yokai or demons for help, she was seeking revenge in every way possible - something she was not unfamiliar with. She had done this in the past multiple times, but never at this level...

She wanted everyone to suffer as much as she did when she lost her son.

Sakura's parents did everything in their power to heal as many villagers as possible; they felt overwhelmed.

It was a never-ending battle.

One of Hira's yokai, Shigeru (the demon that was responsible for Kazuno's wound), was observing all the damage the demons did to the village and its people.

His task was to watch what was happening and return to Hira to put her in theme with everything.

He noticed Sakura's parents helping the villagers.

After watching them for a while, Shigeru returned to Hira to tell her everything bad that was happening in the village.

Hira was very fond of him because she reminded her of the lost son.

Shigeru somehow filled Hira's void, but in a dark, twisted way.

After Shigeru told her everything, Hira ordered the most powerful yokai to curse Sakura's parents into becoming part of the tree of life for eternity; they would never have human form again.

She ordered the demon to curse the wooden bridge that helped the healers to reach the tree; it became full of Tengu's and other dangerous spirits; their purpose was to prevent any villagers from passing the bridge.

Sakura was still a baby when these events happened, but when the girl was old enough, she knew that one day all of the answers to her questions would be revealed…

Chapter 10

Hira's son

Something that Hira did not know about her son, Susumu, was the fact that he was spending time with boys from the other villages who were older than him and had dangerous habits.

These boys had a passion for stealing…

They had stolen things from every house or villager they knew was vacant or too busy to notice their presence.

When they met Hira's son, they knew immediately that he was the type of boy that liked school, but did not have any friends…

The older boys decided to manipulate him into becoming their decoy.

His task was to distract the villager's' attention while the teenagers entered the houses and stole whatever they could find of value or not.

Little did they know that this arrangement they had established would end in a tragedy…

After Hira's son distracted one of the villagers, and the others entered his house, one of the neighbors saw the older boys enter the house, and he knew exactly what was going on…

The neighbor started yelling and the teenagers quickly escaped from the house, took Hira's son with them and started running.

The people from the village ran after them, but the boys were too fast.

They had reached a steep area, full of huge rock formations. Instead of slowing down, they continued to move fast.

Huge mistake…

When Hira's son put his foot on a rock that seemed stable, it cracked, and he collapsed along with the avalanche of rocks.

Because of the fog from that altitude, the boys could not see how deep it was; they started yelling to check if Hira's son was still alive.

No response.

The teenagers assumed he died from the fall.

After this experience, they swore to each other to never steal again from anybody.

They were too traumatized by this event in order to even talk about it.

But as always, the Universe has its own way to put everything in balance.

What would happen to them nobody could have predicted…

Chapter 11

Blood runs thicker than water

Although months had passed after Matsuko sensed the dark energy that was lingering in the air, and things were apparently quiet and peaceful in the village, Sakura's grandparents knew that they could not afford to let their guard down, and at the same time it was vital that they would not disturb the peace in the village until they knew for sure what was really happening.

It was time for Takumi and Matsuko to tell their granddaughter about Shinsei village's dark past, Hira's reign and why she felt so threatened by Sakura's parents.

This made the girl even more determined to find her parents, protect her village and do everything in her power to maintain the peace in her realm.

Chapter 12

Hira and her army of yokai return

Matsuko's worst fear became reality.

Hira was determined to finish what she started.

She knew about Sakura's existence and she wanted to finish her and her legacy.

Hira wanted nothing more than to see Shinsei village and her people disappear for good for the suffering they caused her.

She was so full of poison that she could not accept the fact that it was not the villager's' fault that her son had disappeared from the face of the earth.

Hira went mad completely and there was nothing the villagers could do to stop her, except for one person…

Chapter 13

Sakura leaves the village

Before Sakura left the village, her grandparents told her to take Maru with her on the journey, and to reach the temple located in the mountains, there she would find the first piece of the puzzle to save the village.

Matsuko told the girl to hurry, the time was precious.

The yokai almost destroyed everything in their path, they were more than the last time and the damage they caused was horrendous.

Even though Sakura was stressed about how her grandparents would cope without her help, she knew that in order to have the chance to see them again, she had to save the village.

Although Sakura felt her heart ripped apart, she had to leave.

She took Maru, a bag of food and clothes, and they left…

Chapter 14

Satoru

After a few days of walking in the mountains, Sakura and Maru rested.

The little ball of fur was exhausted, and so was Sakura.

She knew that they had a few hours of sleep until they had to walk again, not to waste the time.

Sakura felt asleep.

The little chinchilla was sleeping on her belly.

During her sleep, Sakura had a vision of a man praying, a river and a bird.

When she woke up from her dream, she knew that the man praying in her dream had to be the man from the temple.

After feeding Maru she ate, put some warmer clothes on, and they continued walking.

At some point they saw a structure in the woods, it was the temple.

They went closer.

Maru got scared from a noise he heard from the tree branches and jumped out of Sakura's bag.

He ran towards the temple and went inside.

Sakura now had another problem up her sleeve, to recover the little bastard…

The walls of the temple were huge.

Sakura wanted to be respectful to the place; she did not want to disturb the people who were praying, but she knew she had to move.

The little rascal found a crack in the wall and went inside.

At some point, a man came out of the temple with her chinchilla.

Sakura felt embarrassed but in the same moment she was glad the little prankster had been recovered thanks to the kind man.

The man, named Satoru, looked Sakura in her eyes and immediately knew who she was and said to the girl, "You are the daughter of Kazuno and Yukimo."

When she heard what the man said, she was shocked.

Sakura had no idea about the connection this man had with her parents and how he knew who she was after only a few seconds.

She asked Satoru, "How do you know my parents? And did you recognize me? I have never seen you before in my life…"

He responded, "Child, I have known your parents since a long time ago.

"Before you were born, your mother was the village's healer as you surely know, she had to pass the wooden bridge that connects all areas of your village.

"Because of the rain that had eaten the old timber, it broke in the moment she was passing it.

"I was near the bridge when I heard your mother scream and I ran to her, grabbed her hand and saved her.

"She did not see who I was."

Sakura thought about what Satoru said and asked him, "But why did you not wish my mother to see you?

"You saved her…"

Satoru responded, "I do not belong to the human world,

child. Only you and your grandmother know of my existence.

"When your father, Kazuno, was passing your region he was attacked by a yokai; he survived the attack and found Shinsei village and here he met your mother; she healed him; you were the result of their love, child".

"Your grandmother prayed that your family and your village would be protected.

When he was healthy, your grandfather came often to the temple to pray, he could not see me; but I always wished that your family would be protected from all evil."

After listening to what Satoru said, Sakura asked him something. His answer would change her life forever.

"But how come only my grandmother and me can see you?"

The man responded, "Child, you and your grandmother are direct 'passage ways', if you like, between the world of the dead and the world of the living.

"You were chosen before you were born to fulfill a prophecy…"

Sakura began questioning if she had not gone mad too, like Hira did.

She asked Satoru, "But why me? What is it about me that made the Universe choose me for this journey?"

The man said, "I cannot give you the answer to this question child. Find the river that flows from the mountain and you will find your answer."

Sakura responded, "I understand. This is a riddle I have to solve in order to save my realm…"

"Indeed. The only thing you have to do, child, is to have the eyes of the mind and soul wide open; and the answer will appear at the right time," Satoru answered.

The entity disappeared.

Chapter 15

Yasuo

Sakura continued her journey with Maru along her side.

The region they had to pass was very dangerous, it was filled with brown bears and black bears.

Even though the girl was scared, she had no other choice but to find the river Satoru told her about.

Soon, she heard the voice of what seemed to be a child playing in the woods.

Maru started squeaking and the little one started to laugh.

He found the little chinchilla quite fun.

The little boy came out of the bushes where he was hiding.

At first, he was startled by Sakura's presence.

He did not know there was also a human there.

The little boy named Yasuo was the entity of an unborn child.

He named himself "Yasuo" to have a sense of belonging, even though he did not have the chance to have human form.

He asked Sakura, "What are you looking for?"

She answered, "I was told to find a river."

"Why do you wish to find this river?" Yasuo asked.

"Because it is a piece of the puzzle I have to solve, in order to save my village, little one," Sakura answered.

"If you grant me with one wish, I will show you where to find the river," Yasuo said.

"What is it that your heart desires little one?" asked Sakura.

"I will give you three elements that will help you find the answer. It is something that all children wish they have when they are little, that not all parents can give them; and that some people hold onto even when they are old," said Yasuo.

Sakura knew immediately what the entity of the little boy wanted; because it was something that she also was very fond of when she was a child, a teddy bear.

Her luck was that she always carried in her bag toys for the village children she healed.

Sakura gave one toy to the child entity.

As childish as this may seem for some people; the idea of receiving a toy had in fact a very deep meaning for the little boy.

It was something he could not ever have because he never reached the world of the living; but every time Yasuo saw people crossing the forest to reach the village, he saw that they brought something for their children whenever they could.

It was a symbol of the life he could not have, but was longing for…

The child entity showed Sakura the path she had to take to reach the river.

Before she continued her journey, Yasuo thanked her for helping him finally have a sense of peace…

Meanwhile, the boys that witnessed Susumu's death had returned already to their village. They were still in shock after what had happened to the boy.

The boys were doing everything they could to forget about the unfortunate event, but their feeling of guilt attracted Shinigami spirits that fed on people's feeling of guilt and they had become hunted by these entities.

The Shinigami spirits were not part of Hira's army of yokai, but for many people, they were just as terrifying. Eventually, they had gone mad because of the infinite guilt they felt for the loss of the boy; they knew his mother had to be looking for him till this day, and still did not find her peace…

They started to blame each other for what happened, and soon enough they had completely lost control of their own bodies and returned to the place where the boy had died. The boys became living spirits haunting the forests surrounding their village…

Chapter 16

The river

Eventually Sakura and Maru found the river Satoru told them about.

It was a marvelous sight for the eyes, the water was crystal clear and filled with petals from the flowers of a tree above the river.

When Sakura touched the water, a gorgeous woman figure came out of it, it was a water entity.

The girl looked at how sublime she looked and in a way she was stunned by her beauty and how pure she looked.

"I was expecting you child!" the water entity said.

"Then you know why I am here…" responded Sakura.

The woman made of water smiled at the girl and said, "I sensed Hira's demons lingering in your region child.

She will not find peace until her son returns to her and the people that are responsible for his death are transformed for a greater good."

Sakura said, "Her yokai made huge damages to the people and to the village.

"What do I have to do to restore peace in my region?" Sakura asked the water entity, named Masumi.

The river entity answered, "Child, first of all you have to know that her son no longer has human form.

"I sensed the moment he disappeared from the world of the

living.

"Second of all, in order to find him, you have to reach the second tree of life (gingko biloba tree).

"The people from your village do not know this, but there is a second tree of life which remained in secrecy for the sole purpose that in case the first one was to be destroyed, lives could be saved with the presence of the second one."

"I understand. But where can I find Hira's son?" asked Sakura.

Masumi answered, "Hira's son is a magpie now.

"You will find him in the land between the two trees of life.

"In order to fulfill the prophecy, you have to convince the magpie to take eight golden leaves from each gingko biloba tree and bring them to the temple.

"But be warned, child! Do not let it convince you of anything else outside your task!

"Do not forget your purpose!" Masumi told Sakura.

"Thank you!" Sakura said to the water entity and then hurried to find the realm between the two trees of life.

Chapter 17

The magpie and the golden leaves

After three days of constant walking, Sakura finally found the land Masumi told her about.

She saw the magpie, named Susumu, standing on a pile full of shiny objects that he had taken from every place he laid his eyes on.

Sakura looked at the pile of shiny objects and was shocked by their number.

The magpie was very fond of everything that glittered in the sunlight.

When Susumu saw Sakura and Maru approaching, he took a gold bracelet in his beak and flew towards Sakura.

Susumu then said, "Darling, this gold bracelet would look so good on your hand! Or would you like a necklace instead?"

Sakura remembered what Masumi warned her about, to not let the magpie convince her of anything else; she had to remain focused on what she had to do.

She told Susumu, "Your collection is truly impressive; but what I am about to tell you, defies everything you ever imagined…

"There is a place where objects shine greater than the sun and stars combined."

The magpie opened its eyes wide and said to Sakura, "Oh, really? And where can I find this marvelous place?"

Sakura knew she had to be very careful with what she

responded, so that the magpie did not sense that in reality she needed its help. She responded, "There is a place in the mountains, a temple.

"But in order to enter it, first you must take eight golden leaves from the two gingko biloba trees and all the treasure will be yours to keep."

Susumu became a bit suspicious, but he thought that for a prize this big it would have been a pity not to see it with its own eyes. The magpie said, "If you defeat the ONI that reigns over this land, I will let you have the mountain of gold I am staying on and also I will find this place you are talking about…"

Before Sakura could respond, a huge red ONI appeared in front of Sakura and Maru.

When the little chinchilla saw how big the demon was compared to him, he became paralyzed with fear.

The huge demon lunged towards them, and Sakura tried to reach her bag for the rice and soybeans (to perform the ritual used for abolishing the ONI), but she slipped…

In that moment, the ONI tried to catch her with his big claws, but then a shadow of a man appeared in front of him; the man attacked the demon with a katana, leaving it with a huge wound on its back.

It was Takumi, Sakura's grandfather that came to help her.

Sakura noticed immediately that there was something changed about him; he looked twelve years younger…

The girl saw the spirit from the temple behind her grandfather; Satoru was helping her grandfather save her from the ONI.

"Child, listen to me! In order to defeat the ONI for good, you have to destroy its third eye…but be careful, they are very fast demons…" said Satoru as if her grandfather were speaking.

The ONI was becoming full of rage because of the wound it had on its back, and began to be more aggressive.

"Maru, we have to hurry! Distract the demon's attention while I prepare my dagger..." said Sakura.

After the girl said this, the little chinchilla started running with lightning speed around the ONI until the only thing it could see was the movements of the little animal.

Meanwhile Sakura took out of her bag a sharp dagger (a weapon that her grandfather gave her to protect herself from predators when she had to pass through the forest) and ran towards the demon.

In that moment, the demon hit Takumi and he flew in the air because of how powerful the ONI was.

This made Sakura even more determined to defeat it.

The ONI started speaking and said to Sakura, "You and your family have been disturbing our presence for too long. Yokai have a longer history on these lands than humans do... so give up child, while you still have time!"

"I will end all of you!" said Sakura referring to the demon kind.

After being shoved and thrown in the air seven times, the girl already knew the taste of the soil.

On the eighth time she got up, ran towards the demon and climbed on its huge body while still running.

Sakura attacked its third eye with the dagger.

Afterwards the ONI fell on the ground and was destroyed for good...

Sakura and Maru rushed towards Takumi.

He was all right; a little dizzy, but all right.

After Satoru made sure Takumi was okay and did not have any serious wounds, he got out of Takumi's body, and shifted from ghost form to human form.

Satoru hugged both of them and afterwards left.

After watching all that happened, the magpie kept his word and flew to the trees of life and took in its beak eight golden leaves from each of them and then flew to the temple of INARI.

Sakura and Maru were behind it.

After Susumu dropped the golden leaves in the temple of INARI, something unexpected happened, a huge wind came and took by surprise Sakura and her little fluffy friend, Maru.

Sakura closed her eyes and waited…

In the precise moment the magpie dropped the golden leaves in the temple, Hira's army of yokai were taken by the wind and disappeared from Shinsei village. Sakura's parents were set free and regained their human form and the boys that were responsible for Susumu's death, that were now entities, were transformed into white foxes that guarded the temple of INARI for eternity.

The village of Shinsei became full of crops and had acres full of rice and all kinds of vegetables that the villagers needed for food.

They never felt hunger ever again.

Finally, Hira was set free from the dark forces that unleashed all the madness and was reunited with her son.

Even though he was still a magpie; Hira did not mind at all.

She finally was at peace, she found her beloved son…

After she recovered Susumu, they left the village of Shinsei for good, in order to start to live a fresh, peaceful life, without bothering any other soul.

Chapter 18

Kazuno, Yukimo and Sakura

Finally, her quest was over.

Sakura not only saved her beloved realm, but also her parents.

She knew that if it had not been for the help of her grandparents, none of this would have been possible…

Sakura had her first family meal with her parents since she had gotten older.

She couldn't have been more grateful.

Her deepest wish came to life thanks to the help of all the souls that helped her fulfill her journey.

Chapter 19

The cherry tree

The villagers and Sakura's family decided to plant a cherry tree to remind them always how blessed they were to have her in their lives.

A few days later Sakura took Maru and went to rest under the cherry tree.

She put her hands on the ground and fell asleep.

When she felt water on her hands she woke up, the water entity came to see her, alongside Satoru and Yasuo.

"Well done, Sakura, you have fulfilled the prophecy; your village is at peace again and so are these souls, Satoru and Yasuo."

Sakura smiled and thanked the water entity for everything.

Sakura never lost her childish innocence and began to teach the new generations how to help humanity through the art of healing the mind, body and soul.

She became a symbol for the people, a symbol of inner balance and infinite kindness.

The first school of healers Shinsei village ever had, was built due to her resilience and burning desire to spread good into the world.

She had fulfilled her destiny and found the true inner peace through her family.

Five years after the school was built, Sakura met TATSUO

and had their first child together, named MIKIO…

Her legacy of bringing blessings into the world never ended…

It was reborn.

www.ingramcontent.com/pod-product-compliance
Lightning Source LLC
LaVergne TN
LVHW041552060526
838200LV00037B/1249